W9-AWQ-985

A Quinn in Need

This book belong

to: Hannah Smith

This book belong

A Quinn in Need

adapted by Jane Mason and Sarah Hines Stephens
based on "Robot Wars" written by Dan Schneider and Steven Molaro
and "Quinn's Alpaca" written Eric Friedman

Based on *Zoey 101* created by Dan Schneider

SCHOLASTIC INC.

New York   Toronto   London   Auckland   Sydney
Mexico City   New Delhi   Hong Kong   Buenos Aires

If you purchased this book without a cover, you should be aware that this book is stolen property. It was reported as "unsold and destroyed" to the publisher, and neither the author nor the publisher has received any payment for this "stripped book."

No part of this work may be reproduced, in whole or in part, stored in a retrieval system, or transmitted in any form or by any means, electronic, mechanical, photocopying, recording, or otherwise, without written permission of the publisher. For information regarding permission, write to Scholastic Inc., Attention: Permissions Department, 557 Broadway, New York, NY 10012.

ISBN-10: 0-439-88257-5
ISBN-13: 978-0-439-88257-6

© 2007 ApolloMedia.

Published by Scholastic Inc.
SCHOLASTIC and associated logos are trademarks and/or registered trademarks of Scholastic Inc.

12 11 10 9 8 7 6 5 4 3 2 1   7 8 9 10 11/0

Printed in the U.S.A.
First printing, February 2007

A Quinn in Need

CHAPTER 1

Big Cookie

It was another gorgeous day at Pacific Coast Academy. Students all over campus were making their way to class or lunch, walking along the palm-lined paths, talking with one another and soaking up the California sunshine.

In the shady grove near the cafeteria, Zoey Brooks and her friends took a load off. They set their stuff on one of the round cement tables and chatted easily about school and homework. And, most important, lunch.

"Oh, man!" Chase Matthews pounded his fists on the table where he had just parked his tray.

"What's wrong?" Zoey asked, wondering why her best guy friend at PCA was so worked up.

"I forgot to get a big cookie," Chase said with a mopey look on his face. He sighed heavily and eyed

1

Zoey's tray at the same time. Who said guys couldn't multitask?

"Can I have half of your big cookie?" he begged, giving her his best puppy-dog look.

"You can't just go back and get one?" Zoey asked, shaking back her shoulder-length blond hair. It kept catching on her new blue sequin-covered tank.

"No, no." Chase shook his hands, palms out, like he was stopping traffic and totally rejecting Zoey's suggestion. There was no way he was going back into the cafeteria. "The line's way too long," he explained.

Lola raised her eyebrows at the curly-haired guy wearing a puka-shell necklace sitting next to her. All this over a cookie? Chase had to be kidding. "I think you can live without a big cookie," she told him calmly.

"No," Chase insisted. "I'll die without a big cookie." It was a rule. Whenever they had big cookies in the cafeteria, he ate one. Usually chocolate chip.

Lola looked closer at her friend. The dude was not kidding. He was seriously losing it over a cookie — and she thought *she* was the dramatic one! Shaking her head, Lola refocused on her lunch, and . . . ew.

A cookie was one thing, a burger was another. And there was something seriously wrong with hers. It had looked fine in the line. Now it looked gross, and cold, and totally unappetizing. Forgetting all about Chase, she took a closer peek under the bun. Yuck. Curling her lip, Lola stood up. "I think I'm going to go get a salad," she said, still grimacing. She turned and, with a swish of her long, dark side-ponytail, she was gone. Chase would just have to work out his cookie issues on his own.

"Hey, why don't you go mooch a big cookie off of one of those guys?" Nicole piped up, pointing at another table where three guys were huddled around a laptop screen. Their lunches were sitting untouched on the table.

Chase turned around to take a look. The guys appeared friendly enough. Kinda geeky, but what did he have to lose? He decided to give it a shot. Heck, for a big cookie he'd give almost anything a shot. "I think I will." Chase smiled as he got to his feet and straightened the striped button-down shirt he was wearing over his tee.

Zoey grinned at Nicole, loving her suggestion. Not only would it get her out of sharing her own big cookie, she'd get to watch Chase make a fool of himself over a dessert. It was better lunchtime entertainment than she had seen in a long while.

Nicole grinned back. Her cheeks were as pink as her T-shirt, beaded necklace, and breezy skirt. She was fully matchy-matchy today, and very pastel, just the way she liked it.

Both girls watched Chase approach the table of guys.

As he closed in on his targeted big cookie, Chase overheard snippets of the guys' conversation. They were nerdier than he'd thought from a distance. Nearing the table, he heard them discussing compression and power train aspect ratios and some other things in Geekish that Chase could not quite understand. He hoped the guys also spoke English.

"Hey, um, that's pretty cool," Chase said, motioning toward the screen they were huddled around. He was hoping flattery would earn him a few points — soften them up before he went in for the kill. "What is that, a game?"

The three nerds all turned and looked at Chase like he was an alien, or worse — an alien emitting a really foul stench. The ringleader, a strawberry-blondish mop-headed kid, practically sneered.

"A game?" he said with disgust.

"He thinks it's a game!" A chubby dude with darker, curly hair started laughing at Chase's faux pas and soon all three of the nerds were giggling madly.

"L-O-L!" the black-haired third geek said, speaking in text code.

These guys were worse off than Chase had thought. And English was definitely not their primary language.

"Totally!" the curly-haired geek slapped five with one of the other guys over the table.

Still at her own table, Zoey took a sip of her Blix and watched the scene play out, narrowing her eyes. She did not like what she was seeing. Nicole was scowling, too.

"This happens to be a schematic representation of our latest warbot," the mop-head geek told Chase. He talked to Chase like he was as clueless as a kindergartner.

Trying hard not to get offended — he still wanted the big cookie — Chase gamely asked, "What's a warbot?"

The nerds had another hearty chuckle at Chase's expense. "Man, is there anything you *do* know?" mop-head asked.

"I know I want your big cookie," Chase said, deadpan. He eyed the chocolate chips and licked his lips. He would suffer any humiliation — well, almost any humiliation — for those chocolaty bits.

That's when the guy with the curly dark hair chimed in. "Warbots are remote-control robots used to fight in competitions," he said condescendingly.

"Which," mop-head added, "PCA has won for the last three years . . . *in a row.*"

Okay. Chase nodded. These dudes were brainiacs. He wasn't questioning that, so what was with the disrespectful tone?

"Thanks to us," curly said as the three nerds all nodded in agreement, celebrating their past victories and obviously believing they were more than all that.

"Cool," Chase said. He had not yet given up on his dessert. And being Logan Reese's roommate for three years in a row had taught him how to butter up big egos to get what he wanted. "What does that do?" He pointed to a corner of the computer screen.

Curly slapped the laptop shut. "Uh, these plans are top secret," he said, giving Chase the evil eye.

"Okay." Chase held his hands up in surrender. "It's not like I'm going to steal them," he said. Couldn't they tell he had no interest — and he had a life?

From the other table, Zoey and Nicole were getting more and more offended for their laid-back friend. Who did those geeks think they were? Chase had been nothing but nice, and they had been nothing but insulting.

"Steal them? You couldn't understand them!" mop-head sneered at Chase.

That was over the line. Zoey was out of her seat and at Chase's side in three seconds.

The nerds kept laughing. "R-O-F-L," the text-code geek hooted, meaning he was virtually "rolling on the floor laughing."

"Any other questions?" Mop-head scowled at Chase, daring him to say more.

"Yeah," Zoey said, staring the geeks down. She definitely had a question. "Why do you guys have to be so rude and obnoxious?" she asked, planting her hands on the waistband of her sequin-hemmed denim skirt.

"Who's that?" the curly geek demanded. He looked from Chase to Zoey and back, waiting for an answer.

"Oh, you see, this is a girl," Chase explained, speaking slowly and putting his hands on Zoey's shoulders. He'd taken all he could, and it was time to turn the tables. "Now, uh, I know that might confuse you since you've probably never been this close to one," he said sarcastically.

"Oh, *yeah?*" curly asked.

"Yeah. Your mom doesn't count," Chase shot back quickly.

"Oh." Curly looked down at the table, busted. He thought he had them on a technicality.

"So you guys think you're so smart because you can build a little robot?" Zoey asked, getting back to the subject at hand.

"No!" the geeks all whined in unison.

"We think we're so smart because you *can't*." Mop-head smiled fakely.

"Boo-ya!" text-head yelled. He thought his buddy had gotten off a real snap. But Zoey wasn't going to let that fly.

"Who says we can't?" She shrugged, making the dorm key she always wore around her neck bob.

Chase recognized the tone in Zoey's voice and was suddenly nervous. All he'd wanted was a cookie, and now Zoey was getting in over her head and pulling him down with her. Zoey was not a girl who backed down from a challenge . . . ever. "All right, uh, let's just go sit down now," he said a little quietly, starting to leave and attempting to drag Zoey with him.

"No!" Zoey pulled him back. "My friends and I can build a robot that could crush your robot," she insisted. She wasn't about to let a bunch of rude geeks show her up.

The geeks laughed like Zoey had just told them a hilarious joke.

Little did they know that Zoey wasn't joking. At all.

"Wait!" Mop-head struggled to catch his breath.

"Hold on. Are you seriously saying that you want to challenge us to a 'bot battle?"

"No," Chase answered quickly, desperately trying to get out of the mess Zoey was leading them into. "We're not."

"Yes, we are!" Zoey contradicted him. Where was Chase's self-respect?

The text geek's eyes got huge. "O-M-G!" he said slowly in disbelief.

"Zoooeey . . ." Chase shuddered, unable to believe what his best friend was saying. Sure, it was hard to be taunted by a bunch of rude nerds. But challenging them in their area of expertise was not the answer. Even he knew that.

Chase's sinking feeling got bigger as he watched the three Geeketeers get to their feet and jubilantly accept the challenge.

"Fine!" text-head said, getting in their faces. "It's O-n."

"One week from today our robot will fight your robot," mop-head shouted.

"In the PCA amphitheater. After school," curly added.

"Three o'clock." Text-head finally managed to say something without spelling it.

"We'll be there," Zoey said, completely confident.

"All official robot war rules and guidelines will apply," mop-head put in threateningly.

"Whatever." Zoey rolled her eyes and shook her head before turning and stomping off, sequins flashing. If these dweebs thought they could intimidate her with their rules and guidelines, they were nuts. She would be schooling them soon enough when she won the 'bot war.

"See ya." Chase shrugged, feeling like they had already lost. This might just be Zoey's worst scheme ever.

"T-T-Y-L," the text-head spelled after him.

The laughter of the nerds echoed in Chase's head as he walked away. He shook his unruly curls, wondering how things had gotten so out of hand. All he'd wanted was a big cookie. . . .

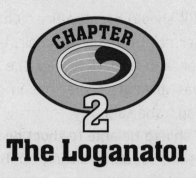

CHAPTER 2

The Loganator

Later that afternoon, on the grassy quad, the reality of what she had gotten them into began to dawn on Zoey. Maybe challenging the nerds to a 'bot war wasn't such a hot idea. Truth be told, none of them had the scientific brainpower or know-how to build a war-bot, much less a winning one.

"Okay, so what else do you think our robot should have?" she asked her crew, trying to look on the bright side. They had a long road ahead and not much time to get there. She was sitting next to Nicole on the pink gingham picnic blanket her roomie had spread on the grass. Behind them, Chase kicked back against a tree. Michael was leaning over his own knees, playing a hand-held video game. Lola sat in a beach chair as she busily sketched out the ideas everyone was throwing out. And Logan? He was working hard — on his tan.

"I think it should breathe fire," Chase offered.

From her rainbow-striped chair, Lola grabbed a nearby marker and added fire to the giant concept sketch she was making of the 'bot in question. "Fire breathing. Okay," she said.

"And it should be able to shoot heat-seeking missiles," Logan said, suddenly sitting up. He adjusted his shades before lying back down on his towel next to the boom box to grab a few more rays.

"Heat-seeking missiles," Lola repeated, furrowing her brow beneath her cute flowered hair clip. These were some tall orders, and Lola was glad she only had to do an artist's rendering — not actually create the machine.

"Ooh!" Michael was suddenly hit by a brain wave and stopped playing his game long enough to add his two cents. "We should rig it up with a microphone and a speaker so we can talk smack to the other robot," he suggested.

"Okay," Zoey agreed. These were all good ideas, but . . . was she the only one who was starting to worry?

Next to Zoey, Nicole was eagerly nodding her approval. She grinned before taking a sip of her water. She had no idea what Zoey was looking so worried about. This was going great!

"Microphone. Smack," Lola said to herself as she added to her drawing.

"What are we going to call our robot?" Chase wondered aloud.

Logan pulled himself back out of his sun soak to make a suggestion. "Let's call it the Loganator."

"Okay, why are you here again?" Lola asked, giving Logan a glare. Leave it to Logan to want the robot named after him!

"Well, someone's gotta pay for the 'bot," Chase explained in a resigned voice. Logan could pretty much get his dad to pay for anything — including a robot that was being built only so it could be destroyed.

"And since I'm paying? We're calling it the Loganator," Logan said decisively before sinking back onto his towel.

"Fine." Zoey rolled her eyes. She was not about to get into it with Logan . . . again. She had gotten into enough stuff today. "Lola, let's see the Loganator," she suggested.

Lola spun her huge pad around to reveal a sharp-looking, fire-shooting, smack-talking blue-and-yellow 'bot.

"Whoa!" Nicole was impressed. She nodded her head approvingly.

The rest of the group chimed in their approval. The 'bot actually looked really fierce!

"Cool!"

"All right!"

"We are going to destroy those little science geeks with that 'bot," Nicole squealed excitedly.

"Yeah," Zoey agreed, not sounding even remotely convinced. "Just one little problem," she pointed out. The one little problem that had been tormenting her since she walked away from the geeks at their lunch table . . .

"What?" Chase asked, already knowing the answer.

Zoey threw up her hands. "None of us knows how to build it!"

Luckily for Zoey, the answer to her problem was sitting on a bench with a sweeping view of the ocean, using an electron microscope to get up close and personal with a piece of lettuce. She was dressed in a long-sleeve T-shirt that was the same color as the ocean behind her and decorated with a bright yellow bird and a design down one sleeve. Her multicolored hair hid several small, decorative braids tied off with purple feathers. PCA's girl genius had more than smarts. She had her own wild fashion sense to boot.

"Hey, Quinn!" Zoey called, hoping to find her

friend in a good mood. Sometimes, like when an experiment was not going well, Quinn could be a little, well, testy. "Whatcha doin' there?" Zoey asked, hoping it was a good idea to find out.

"I'm just making sure my lunch is clean," Quinn explained. She removed her lettuce and reinserted it into her sandwich before wiping her hand on her multi-colored skirt. "People don't always wash lettuce as well as they should," she informed Zoey. "So, what's up?"

"Well," Zoey said slowly as she took a seat on the bench next to her friend. "I was wondering if you would want to help us with a little project."

"Sure. What's the project?" Quinn asked, squinting at Zoey through her square-framed glasses. She hoped it had something to do with science.

"Well, see, we're building this remote-control robot that we're going to use to fight against —"

"Oh, sorry," Quinn interrupted. "I can't help you." She shrugged before taking a huge bite of her sandwich.

Zoey was baffled. How could Quinn blow her off so quickly? She hadn't even listened to the idea yet. "But you just said you'd love to help." She waited anxiously for Quinn to finish chewing so she could answer her. It seemed to take forever.

"I really would like to help. But I just don't believe

in using my gift of science for violence," Quinn said matter-of-factly. She felt pretty strongly about it. After all, look what happened to her hero Einstein. He hadn't really meant to create nuclear weapons. . . . And what about Nobel? He had always regretted the whole dynamite thing.

"Oh, come on!" Zoey couldn't believe it. She knew Quinn had a lot of crazy ideas, but objecting to 'bot wars? The fighting was going to take place between two machines, not living creatures. "It's not *really* violence," Zoey said. "Think of it more like, like two machines just . . . gently . . . crushing each other. To the death." Okay, so maybe it did sound a little violent.

"Sorry." Quinn shook her head again. "I just wouldn't feel right about it." She took a sip of her Blix. As far as she was concerned, the case was closed.

Zoey bit her lip. There had to be a way to convince Quinn. They needed her!

Just then the three 'bot geeks walked up. When they spotted Zoey talking to Quinn, they stopped and stared.

"Uh-oh! Don't tell us you got Quinn to help you build your 'bot!" one of them said, eyeing the girls derisively.

"Now we're really scared!" another said in a high, whiny voice. The three geeks laughed.

Quinn glared at the three boys standing in front of her. "Neil. Andrew. Wayne." She spoke the boys' names slowly and with complete disdain. The mere act of saying the names of these nerds left a bad taste in her mouth.

"Still mad, Quinn?" Neil, the shaggy ringleader, taunted.

"Just 'cause we wouldn't let you join the science club?" Andrew, the curly-haired kid, mocked.

Zoey was totally baffled. "Why wouldn't you let her join?" she asked. Quinn was a whiz at science and a great person, too. Everyone knew that.

"'Cause girls and science go together like sodium hydrochloride and ammonia," Neil spat.

Whatever that meant.

"L-O-L!" Wayne guffawed. The geeks slapped hands.

"Oh, yeah?" Quinn was on her feet, the purple feathers on the ends of her braids flying. "We'll just see who's L-O-L-ing when our 'bot kicks your 'bot's butt into the next millennium."

Zoey could barely believe her ears — or her luck.

The geeks were doing her a huge favor. She stood up next to Quinn. "So you're going to help us?" she asked, amazed.

"Oh, I'm helping you!" Quinn confirmed.

"Whatever," Neil said, acting like it was no big deal. Then he turned and looked Zoey dead in the face. "You can't beat us no matter who helps you," he sneered. "C'mon, guys."

"T-T-Y-L," the text-head smirked.

"B'bye, *Wayne*!" Zoey called after the acronym-happy nerd.

Wayne, who obviously hated his name, scrambled back angrily. "It's Firewire!" he said, planting his face about two inches from Zoey's and telling her his self-chosen nickname.

"C'mon," his nerd friends said, keeping him at bay by holding his backpack straps and leading him away.

"Wayne!" Zoey called after him. Now it was her turn to laugh. She and Quinn giggled together as Wayne was dragged off, choking on a frustrated scream.

CHAPTER 3

Dorkon

Once Quinn was on the job, there was no stopping her. She was a 'bot-building machine! While the rest of the gang loafed around on the couches and beanbags in Brenner lounge, Quinn soldered, and hammered, and connected wires. She had the framing completed, the motor was in, and she was almost done with the speakers and microphone.

"You sure you don't want us to help you build the 'bot?" Zoey asked, setting aside her magazine to check on Quinn's progress.

"Nah." Quinn didn't even look up from the part she was attaching. "You'll just slow me down," she said distractedly. She couldn't wait to see the looks on the faces of her enemy when her team's creation tore theirs to bits.

Zoey turned back to Nicole, who was sitting next

to her on the polka-dot couch, flipping through her own mag. "I think we were just insulted," she said lightly.

Nicole nodded once, agreeing. "It was subtle, but yes." Not that she minded. She didn't really want to get any axle grease on her paisley-print Bermuda shorts or hot-pink satin jacket.

"There." Quinn lifted her safety goggles up to her forehead. "I just finished the onboard speaker so you boys can do your smack talk," she said with a grin.

"Ooh!" That got Chase's attention. He jumped right out of his bright yellow beanbag chair. "I want to try," he said as he rushed over.

Quinn handed Chase a microphone. Chase took it and flipped it over in the air, caught it easily, switched it on, and waited for the feedback to die down.

"I am a robotic killing machine," Chase said into the mic. But the voice that came out was not Chase's. It was mechanized and sounded a little scary. "Prepare to meet your doom," he went on. Logan and Michael stopped tossing the Frisbee they were playing with to listen. Nicole, Zoey, and Lola got up off the couches, too. The 'bot voice sounded awesome!

"Do not be fooled by my pathetic name, the Loganator!" Chase joked. The whole gang, except Logan, cracked up.

"Ha-ha-ha," Logan said as they all gathered around the wire- and part-covered table where Quinn had been working.

Nicole looked down at the cobalt-blue robot. "You know," she said, staring at the sleek machine, "I don't think our 'bot looks intimidating enough." It was actually pretty cute.

"Yeah," Michael had to agree. "It needs a big ol' Mohawk, like this high." He held his hand up to the top of Lola's and Zoey's heads. "That would really kick up the intimidation factor."

Everyone nodded. A giant Mohawk *would* make their 'bot scarier. . . .

Chase shook his head thoughtfully and picked up a thick book. He recalled reading something about robot height. "Uh, according to the interscholastic robot guidelines, the height of a 'bot cannot exceed thirty-six inches. So, if we add a big Mohawk, we could get disqualified," he said, confirming his thought before slamming the book shut. Ixnay on the ohawkmay.

"That's right," Logan said.

Quinn put down her tools and surveyed her work. She was barely listening to what the others were saying. Her mind was already moving on to the next task. "Okay, I'll be back," she told the group.

"Where you going?" Zoey asked. They were making good progress. She didn't want Quinn to quit now.

"To get another gainsley sprocket," Quinn said, as if it should be obvious to everyone what was necessary to keep working.

"Hmmm." Lola nodded knowingly and crossed her arms over her green embellished tank. She had no idea what Quinn had just said, but it sounded good.

With Quinn gone, everyone leaned in to take a closer look at the mass of parts and wires that was coming together to make their 'bot.

"Man, we are lucky we have Quinn," Zoey said, eyeing the tiny wires and metal pieces. She would never be able to make sense out of this stuff.

"We *so* couldn't have built this thing without her," Nicole agreed.

"Yeah, it's good we got our own geek," Logan put in.

Nicole made a face, and Zoey turned around to give Logan a look. "Logan . . . ." she said. Did the guy not have a single sensitive bone in his body?

"Dork?" Logan tried.

"Dude!" Chase reprimanded his roomie, "That is not nice."

Logan grabbed the microphone. Who needed nice

when you could be funny? "I am Quinn," he said in the robotic voice. "I must go get a sprocket from my home planet, Dorkon."

Zoey couldn't help it. She laughed. Logan was a jerk, but he could make a good joke. Lola and Nicole cracked up, too.

"I am Quinn, from Dorkon," Logan went on until he had the whole room rolling on the floor.

Then suddenly Quinn appeared in the doorway. Her braceleted wrist was on her hip, and her eyes flashed angrily. "So, you guys think I'm a dork?" she said hotly.

The room was silent. Nicole bit her lip.

Zoey tried to explain. "Quinn, we were just —"

"Making fun of me?" Quinn asked, sounding hurt.

Chase tried to explain. "Look, Logan was just —"

"I heard what he was doing," Quinn interrupted. "And I heard you *all* laughing. Look, if you all think I'm such a dork, you can just finish your stupid robot on your own." Quinn's voice was shaking. As she pulled off her goggles, she had to blink back tears. All her hard work, and this was the thanks she got? Tossing her goggles on the floor, Quinn spun in her pink high-top sneakers and stomped out.

Nobody knew what to say. Zoey felt terri~~ble. She~~ hadn't really meant to laugh . . . but . . .

The sound of Quinn's dorm room door slamming echoed down the hall and made Zoey flinch.

"Uh-oh," Logan said into the robot mic. Zoey grabbed a pillow and chucked it at him, knocking him off the back of the couch. Logan didn't know when to stop. And she wished he had never started.

Shocking Apology

The sign on the door read QUINN=MC². The science girl's favorite formula. Zoey knocked gingerly. She had a lot of apologizing to do. "Quinn?" she called. "Quinn, I know you're in there. Please open the door. Please? We're sorry."

"Go away!" a sad voice answered from the other side.

"Come on. That was just Logan being a jerk," Zoey explained. "It's what he does." It was totally true, but Zoey still felt bad.

Suddenly a little door above the Quinn sign opened and Quinn's face appeared. "I expect to be made fun of by Logan," she said. "What I didn't expect was for everyone to laugh. Especially you. I thought you were my friend." Quinn's framed face looked completely crushed.

"I am," Zoey said. Quinn's voice was trembling and Zoey would have given anything to take the whole thing back. The last thing she ever wanted was to hurt Quinn. "Sometimes friends make mistakes," Zoey explained.

"Clearly," Quinn said before slamming the little door shut.

"Quinn, will you please come down to the lounge with me?" Zoey pleaded.

"You don't want me — you just want my brain to finish your precious warbot," Quinn yelled through the door.

Breathing a heavy sigh, Zoey decided she had to talk to Quinn face-to-face, whether she wanted to or not. She simply had to convince her friend that she really *was* her friend. But the second she grasped the metal door handle, Zoey felt a strong jolt travel up her arm. "Ow! Quinn, did you electrify this door-knob?" she asked, shaking some feeling back into her hand.

"If you're not sure, why don't you try touching it again?" Quinn suggested. Zoey could hear just a touch of evil scientist in her voice. A mad Quinn was not something you wanted to mess with. No, the best choice was to leave Quinn alone for a while so she could cool off.

"No thanks, I'm good," Zoey answered, still shaking her arm. But as she walked away, she realized that she was not good at all. She felt horrible.

"I feel so bad about Quinn," Nicole said later that afternoon. She, Zoey, and Lola were walking to class slowly.

"We just need to apologize like a thousand more times and she'll be okay . . . in a week or two," Zoey said. If electrifying her door was a sign, it would probably take at least a week or two for Quinn to forgive them.

"Guess we can forget about beating those science geeks," Lola said dejectedly.

"Yeah, I'll just have to tell them we're forfeiting," Zoey said, totally bummed. She'd really been looking forward to putting those jerks in their place. But losing the 'bot challenge was nothing compared to losing a friend.

"Hey, guys!" Chase yelled down to the girls from the walkway by the lounge. "You better come see this."

"See what?" Zoey asked. They had a class to get to, and cutting class at PCA was a serious no-no.

"Just hurry!" Chase said. He didn't look like he was joking around.

Zoey looked at the other girls and they hurried up to Chase and into the building.

In the lounge, PCA news was blaring on the big screen. Jeremiah, the PCA anchor, was reporting breaking news, live.

"...And I've just learned that the PCA science club's battling robot, which usually competes against other schools, will be fighting the robot of fellow PCA student Zoey Brooks," Jeremiah reported.

Zoey looked at Nicole. Her roommate's eyes were wide. Her mouth was hanging open. She looked as nervous and scared as Zoey felt. Two seconds ago they'd been ready to call the whole thing off. Now it was the big news on campus.

"Is that true, Neil?" Jeremiah held the microphone so Neil could answer. He was standing on the lawn with his remote in his hand. Wayne and Andrew were standing with him.

"Yeah, it is, Jeremiah," Neil answered. "Zoey and her friends said they could build a 'bot that could beat our 'bot."

"L-O-L." Wayne laughed dorkily.

"So this Friday, we'll just see." Andrew leaned in for a little mic time.

"Great! So, is this your 'bot?" Jeremiah looked at the small metal box on the sidewalk and the camera panned down. The 'bot had twin saw blades in the front and flames emblazoned on its sides. The inner workings of the robot were still visible, but it looked almost complete.

"Yep. Sure is. It's not done yet, but it will be soon," Neil said ominously.

"And it'll crush any 'bot that dares to attack it," Andrew added.

"Yeah. And to demonstrate? We've got this doll that happens to look a lot like Zoey!"

Neil was getting more and more excited as he spoke. In fact, the whole science club was looking seriously scary as they dropped the small blond doll on the sidewalk.

While Zoey watched, Neil piloted the 'bot, forcing it to run over her plastic likeness again and again, dragging the doll by her hair in circles while the science geeks laughed.

"That's what we're going to do to Zoey's 'bot this

Friday," Neil said into the camera when the horror show was through.

"Yeah, be there," Andrew shouted, like it was a wrestling match.

"Yeah, says *Firewire*," Wayne added. He puffed out his chest for emphasis.

"Quit that," Neil whispered harshly at Wayne.

Jeremiah stepped in front of the frothing nerds. "For PCA news, I am Jeremiah Trottman," he said, signing out.

"Oh my god." Chase snapped off the set, silencing the maniacal laughter of the geeks.

"Well, that's it, we can't quit now," Zoey said, crossing her arms over her PCA baseball T-shirt. There was no way she could let those nerds humiliate them in front of the whole school.

"We have to," Lola said, flopping down next to Zoey on the couch. "Other than those science geeks, Quinn's the only one who can finish building our 'bot!" She played with her bright beaded choker nervously.

"No she's not," Chase said, holding up a finger. He had an idea, and it was not a bad one, if he did say so himself. "I think we need to pay a little visit to Miles

Brody," he explained, sitting down on the coffee table in front of the girls.

Zoey, Lola, and Nicole all looked at one another, confused. "Who's Miles Brody?" Nicole asked.

"The number one smartest guy at PCA . . . *ever*," Chase explained. If anyone could help them Miles could.

"Well, where do we find him?" Zoey asked, exasperated. She was desperate. Which meant she was open to anything.

"That's easy," Chase said.

The mood as they entered the Harry Schneider Library was somber, almost spooky. Zoey followed Chase through the shelves of books, feeling nervous. She needed this plan to work.

Then they spotted him. Miles Brody was sitting in a leather chair reading a hardcover book. On the table next to him were a lamp, a bottle of water, and a plate of cut-up vegetables complete with dip. Obviously the guy was feeling right at home in this corner of the library.

Chase, Zoey, and Nicole stopped in front of his chair. Miles looked up at them through his round spectacles.

"Hello," he greeted them. Zoey noticed he had an accent, but couldn't tell where it was from. The guy looked smart, at least. She hoped Chase was on to something here.

"Hey, Miles, uh, listen . . ." Chase began smoothing his green-and-gray polo shirt. "Sorry to bug you, but, uh —"

"Please, allow me to finish my book before we speak," Miles said drily.

Zoey eyed the remaining fifty or so pages of Miles's book. She hoped he wasn't really going to make them stand there for the half hour it would take for him to read to the end. But much to her amazement, Miles thumbed through the pages, skimming each one in about two seconds.

"My book is done," he said, closing the book in less than a minute.

This could be the guy, all right. Zoey started to introduce herself to the dude who could save the day. "So, um, my name's —"

"Your name is Zoey Brooks," Miles finished, helping himself to a carrot stick.

"Yeah, how did you know?" Zoey asked, shocked.

"Your dormitory is Brenner Hall. You were born

in the South, specifically a small town in Louisiana whose name I know, but it is not significant so I'll keep it to myself." Miles twirled his carrot as he spoke and seemed to enjoy the surprised looks on their faces. "You enjoy athletics, e.g., basketball, and you maintain a three-point-eight-five grade point average. Impressive . . . to most."

"Told ya," Chase said, raising his eyebrows. Miles was a little weird, but he was their man. "He knows everything."

"Is this about your 'bot fight?" Miles asked. "I assume I'm correct, am I?"

"What are you, like psychic or something?" Nicole asked, her brown eyes wide.

Miles smiled at Nicole, amused. "Sadly there is no such ability, but you are cute to assume such."

"So, uh, how did you know about the 'bot war?" Chase asked.

"This entire school has been made aware of your looming robot battle and the involvement of one Miss Zoey Brooks." Miles turned his bespectacled gaze back to Zoey. He was smiling slightly and seemed to be enjoying himself.

Only how did he know who she was and why she

was there? Zoey wondered, and decided to ask. "Yeah, but how —"

"Then a girl approaches me with a key around her neck bearing the letter Z, as in Zoey. And since I am familiar with the abilities of PCA's fine science club, and since you are amateurs, I imagine that at this point you're growing nervous about your impending battle so you have come to me for advice and/or assistance. Am I correct?" Miles asked.

Zoey stopped listening about halfway through Miles's little speech. He was starting to creep her out. "Um, I just want you to help us," she said plainly. "Will ya?"

Miles hesitated. He set down his carrot and looked at them over the tops of his glasses. "Yes I will," he said.

"Really?" Zoey could barely believe it. Nicole practically started jumping up and down.

"On one condition," Miles added.

"Sure. What?" Zoey shrugged. "Just tell me."

Taking a sip of water, Miles fixed Zoey with his stare. "Make them go away first," he said, lifting a pale finger toward Chase and Nicole.

Definitely weird, but Zoey was desperate. She looked over at Chase and Nicole, who promptly wandered off.

"Okay. What's your condition?" Zoey asked when they were gone.

"I'll help you with your robot," Miles began as he got to his feet. He was taller than Zoey and had a funny look in his eyes. "But in return I would like a date," he said, raising his brows.

"Um . . ." Zoey was not sure how she was going to let this brainiac down easily. "Well, I'm flattered and all —"

"Not with you," Miles said flatly. "With your delightful friend. The perky brunette in the fuchsia blouse?"

Zoey turned to see where Miles was looking. He was staring at Nicole, who was perched on a shelf checking her face in a compact, totally oblivious.

This was a problem. No way was Miles Nicole's type. Besides, she wasn't accustomed to accepting dates for her friends.

"I can't promise you a date with Nicole," Zoey said, exasperated. That would be worse than going out with Miles herself — well, almost.

"How unfortunate." Miles turned away and went back to his chair.

"Look, can't we just buy you a big dictionary or

something?" Zoey asked. What did über-smart kids do for fun, anyway?

"You know what I want and I will not settle for less. If you want my help on your 'bot, then guarantee me a date with your friend." Miles's tone was final. If there had been any other way, she would have taken it. But there wasn't. It was Miles's way or the highway.

"Okay," Zoey agreed, hoping Nicole would forgive her when she found out. "If you help us with our 'bot, I promise you a date with Nicole," she said, frowning.

Miles grinned. "Fabulous."

CHAPTER 5

Miles to Go

Miles rolled up the sleeves of the button-down shirt he wore under his sensible sweater vest, adjusted his goggles, and got to work.

Zoey watched from a safe distance. She did not want to mess up her layered peach-and-turquoise tanks with solder burn holes. And to tell the truth, Miles kind of freaked her out. She was not sure how she was going to explain to Nicole that she had auctioned off some time with her to the King of Geeks. Fortunately — or unfortunately — she didn't have much time to think about it.

Miles pulled off his goggles and looked at the robot crew.

"Well?" Zoey prompted him. Was there a problem?

"Your 'bot is completed according to your directions and specifications," Miles said smugly.

It was music to everyone's ears.

"All right!"

"Yay!"

"Awesome!"

The whole gang yelled and cheered. Even Logan.

"Yes, yay," Miles said evenly. "Now, who will be your operator?" He eyed each of them skeptically.

Zoey looked at Nicole, who looked at Lola, who looked at Michael, who looked at Chase, who shrugged and looked back at Zoey. "Um. I guess me," she said, unsure.

Zoey's friends grinned and nodded. It sounded good to them!

"Then please, pay attention." Miles stepped around the table he had been using as a workbench and held up a large remote control. "Left. Right. Forward. Reverse." He rapidly operated a little toggle on the right side of the remote. "Flip. Thrust. Twirl. Strike. That is all."

Miles was talking so fast, Zoey wasn't sure she caught any of it, let alone all of it. She looked at Nicole nervously. Maybe she could get in a little practice time.

"Come on, guys, the fight starts in fifteen minutes," Michael announced.

Or not.

"All right! Let's go kick some 'bot!" Chase pumped the air and then rubbed his palms together in anticipation.

Everyone cheered, and then Michael and Chase carefully lifted their blue-and-white robot off the table and headed for the door. Zoey grabbed the remote and started to follow her friends, but Miles called her back.

"Zoey, don't forget about our arrangement. My date with your friend Nicole? Tomorrow night." Miles raised his eyebrows behind his glasses.

"I won't," Zoey said. How could she? She had been dreading telling Nicole ever since she made the desperate promise. "You just be ready," Zoey said, backing away.

"I shall bathe like I've never bathed before," Miles said with a dreamy look in his eye.

Zoey tried to block out the icky mental image. "Lucky Nicole," she said. She hoped she did not sound as afraid as she felt as she backed out of the room.

She would think about Miles and his date later. Right now she had a battle to win.

*   *   *

"Hey, here they come!"

At least half the school had gathered on the benches that surrounded the sunken amphitheater to see the robot battle take place on the stage below. When word started to spread that Zoey and her team were on their way, the crowd went nuts.

"Fight! Fight! Fight!" they chanted as Michael, Chase, and the 'bot came into view.

"That's their 'bot?" Neil wrinkled up his face in amusement at the Loganator.

"Lame!" Andrew said.

"R-O-F-L!" Wayne held up his hand for a high five. Andrew slapped his hand and the whole geek squad laughed hysterically.

The crowd continued to chant as Zoey took her place at the base of the stairs. Lots of the kids were cheering for her crew. But some of them were definitely on the science club's side.

Taking a deep breath, Zoey looked at the controls and tried to remember what Miles had said. *Right. Left. Forward. Reverse. Flip. Thrust. Twirl. Strike.* She could do this. She had to. Her reputation depended on it.

The geeks looked confident as the robots started to roll into the center of the paved circle. Their completed 'bot looked tough. It had three sets of spinning, red-tipped saw blades on its back. The base was painted with fierce-looking flames. And sometime since the news brief, it had been fitted with a ramming arm that was finished with nasty red metal spikes that could be raised up and brought crashing down.

By comparison, the Loganator was kind of cute. It looked more like a sports car, with a tiny prod on one side, a spinning rotor on top, and a racing stripe down the middle.

"You sure you want to fight?" Wayne asked. "'Cause you can walk away right now with your pretty little 'bot."

"Before we crush it to death," Neil added with a sneer.

Zoey glared at the nerds. Wayne was laughing, hard. He had his polo shirt buttoned all the way up to his neck. Who did he think he was talking to?

"Come on, let's fight!" Zoey yelled, working the throng of kids into a frenzy.

Chase and Michael pumped their fists in the air and chanted with the crowd. Nicole jumped up and down, clapping. The mood was intense as the 'bots rolled toward each other, and then —

"Hold it! Hold it!" There was a yell from the top of the stairs. A bald-headed man in a yellow tie and dark jacket was running toward the fight, waving his arms. "Stop the fight!" he ordered.

"Teacher!" a kid in a striped PCA jersey hissed.

"It's the dean of science!" Michael said through clenched teeth.

"This is bad," Logan said, ducking his head. He did not want to get in trouble over this silly geek war.

"No," Chase assured Zoey and the rest of his friends, "this is awesome. He'll stop the fight and we won't have to lose in front of the whole school."

Zoey began to nod. Chase had a point. As much as she wanted to teach these jerks a lesson, she had a feeling they were going to lose, big time. This could be their out!

"Oh, thank goodness the fight hasn't started yet," the science dean said, stopping next to Chase on the stairs. His voice was filled with relief.

"So, I guess you're shutting us down," Chase said, trying hard to sound disappointed.

"Are you kidding?" the teacher asked. "I have been waiting all week for this!" He looked at the crowd and began to chant, urging them to join in. "Fight! Fight! Fight!"

It was on again. There was no backing out now.

Zoey bent over her controls. All around her,

people were yelling and screaming. The flame-covered 'bot was moving in fast.

"Go get 'em, Zo'!" Chase cheered enthusiastically.

"I'll try," Zoey said as her hands worked the levers. She managed to get in the first good ram. The geeks' 'bot was big, but it was slower. Zoey chased it down and rammed it again before they managed to turn and strike back. They traded bashes evenly for a while, then a head-on collision sent Zoey's 'bot into a spin.

At the controls of the geek 'bot, Neil laughed like a madman and went in for the kill. He rammed Zoey's dizzy 'bot, ripping a hole in the outer shell. Sparks flew. The little blue 'bot made a terrible noise, and when Zoey tried to turn and retaliate, her remote did not respond. The 'bot spun out of control.

"Come on!" Logan said impatiently.

"Hit him back," Michael yelled.

"Do you not see me pressing buttons here?" Zoey asked, feeling exasperated. Did they think she liked being a sitting duck? It wasn't working!

"Come on, dude," Andrew said from across the amphitheater. "Quit messing around and finish them off."

Neil swung the geek 'bot around. "No problem," he said cockily. "Check this out!" He manipulated his controls and the geek 'bot's large crushing arm raised up to its full height. The red spikes looked like sharp, jagged teeth as it began to approach the disabled blue 'bot.

"Uh-oh," Chase said. He could hardly look.

Uh-oh was right. Zoey stood helpless as the menacing 'bot prepared to slam hers. All she could do was watch as the toothy arm crashed down, piercing the blue metal shell and frying the electronics inside.

The crowd went nuts. The science team jumped around, celebrating.

Nicole refused to believe it was all over. "Fight back!" she screamed.

"I can't. It's dead." Zoey pushed buttons and pulled levers, to no avail. The 'bot wasn't moving.

In the center of the arena, their unresponsive little blue 'bot continued to sizzle and send up smoke.

"It looks like we have a winner!" The dean of science was jumping around more than the kids. He could barely contain himself.

"Boo-ya!" Andrew cheered himself. Some of the crowd booed the brutal winners.

"We lost," Michael said, disappointed.

"Well, how could we win when they have that huge hammer thing?" Chase wanted to know.

Zoey looked at the giant, toothy arm still imbedded in their 'bot.

Behind her, Lola started to smile. "Hey, remember what you said about the Mohawk?" she asked, her dark eyes sparkling almost as much as her shiny beaded necklaces and sequin-trimmed crocheted top.

"What'd I say?" Chase asked, not remembering. Whatever it was, he hoped it was good.

"The rules," Lola said, waiting for them to get on the same page she was on. "A 'bot can't be over thirty-six inches tall." She gestured toward the geek 'bot.

Of course! Chase and Zoey exchanged looks, and for the first time they were happy to have adhered to "all official robot war rules and guidelines."

CHAPTER 6

And the Winner Is . . .

A few minutes later, the dean of science was kneeling beside the 'bots in the amphitheater and squinting at a tape measure.

"Well?" Zoey was dying to know how the giant arm measured up.

"With the hammer up, it's thirty-nine inches, which is over the limit," the dean confirmed.

The crowd, which had also been waiting for the verdict, cheered along with Zoey and her friends.

Neil turned to Wayne and glared. "Nice going, *Firewire*," he shouted sarcastically.

"So does this mean we win?" Zoey asked.

The dean shook his head. "No. But the rules state that you can have a rematch, and they can't use the hammer this time."

Zoey, Lola, and Nicole looked at the bickering science club geeks. They crossed their arms, daring them with a look.

"We can win *without* the hammer," Neil said, glaring back at the girls.

"So, you losers want a rematch, or what?" Andrew asked.

Zoey looked to the boys who were crouched behind her, huddled over their 'bot assessing the damage. "Guys?" she inquired.

"Too much damage," Chase said, peering up through a cloud of smoke.

"Too much damage," Andrew giggled proudly.

Chase shook his head. "This thing can't fight."

The geeks giggled victoriously again.

Then, silent as a cat, Quinn appeared. She stood in the amphitheater with her hands behind her back. "Mine can," she said calmly.

"Quinn." Neil wheeled around. "Don't tell me *you* built a 'bot."

"That's right," Quinn said. She pulled a tiny purple robot from behind her back and placed it on the ground. It was less than half the size of the other 'bots. A small half-circle on wheels, Quinn's robot was emblazoned with a red *Q*. It had four tiny flashing lights and was armed with only one small cannon.

"O-M-G," Wayne exclaimed.

Andrew could not contain his laughter.

"See? This is exactly why girls don't belong in the science club," Neil said, shaking his head over the ador-able 'bot.

"You wanna talk or fight?" Quinn demanded. Her calm was gone, replaced by a low burning anger.

Lola, Zoey, and Nicole watched the exchange, lov-ing it. Quinn was back and she was powerful mad — and not just at them!

"Let's fight!" Andrew shouted.

"Let's go, yeah."

"Do it!"

"Fight!"

The crowd rushed to find their seats in the stands and take up the chant. "Fight! Fight! Fight!" they yelled in unison.

Quinn calmly held her teeny remote. It had a joy-stick, an antenna, and a single red button. The zippy little purple 'bot wheeled across the amphitheater and boldly stopped in front of the big red-toothed 'bot wrecker.

The geeks laughed. Why had Quinn even bothered? They could crush her 'bot like a tiny purple bug!

Zoey looked at Chase. She wondered what Quinn was thinking. It didn't look like she stood a chance. Chase didn't look too sure, either.

Then, with the touch of a button, Quinn's tiny 'bot made a spacey noise. A blue ball of energy grew at the tip of its teensy cannon and suddenly shot out.

Kaboom!

The ball of energy found its mark, and the science club's robot flew into flaming bits and lay, smoldering and shattered, on the concrete.

The crowd screamed, shielding themselves from the flying debris. Then they were silent.

Zoey was the first person to speak. "Wow!" she exclaimed.

"O-M-G," Wayne reacted in geek speak. He sounded like he was about to cry. Neil and Andrew were speechless.

"Thanks for playing," Quinn said sweetly, giving her rivals a little wave.

"All right!" Chase came rushing over to congratulate Quinn.

"Unbelievable!"

"You're the best!" Zoey and her friends shouted as they surrounded the winner.

Quinn's momentary look of happiness vanished. She looked down at her lacy red spaghetti-strap tank.

"We totally owe you!" Logan said, patting Quinn on the back.

"I only did it because I couldn't stand to see those jerks win," Quinn said sullenly. "Nobody owes me anything." Quinn shook off the other kids and took the steps down to the amphitheater floor two at a time to collect her 'bot.

"But Quinn . . ." Nicole tried to stop her.

"Wait up," Chase called.

But Quinn didn't even turn around.

Later that night, Quinn lay on the floor of her dorm room. Her head was propped on a pillow and she was wondering why her victory was not so sweet. She'd thought it would feel awesome to take those annoying geeks and their 'bot down. But it only left her feeling . . . hollow.

There was a knock at her door.

"Go away," Quinn called. Another knock. Ugh. Didn't they get the message? Rolling onto her hands and knees, Quinn got to her feet and yanked open her door. "I said go away!" she yelled at . . . nobody. The hall was empty. Then she heard something. Beeping.

The blue-and-white Loganator was idling in the hall. It was cleaned and repaired, and on its back was a vase full of cheery yellow tulips. The flowers bobbed as the robot rolled into the room and stopped in the center.

"Okay. What's going on?" Quinn wondered aloud.

"We're sorry, Quinn," the robot said in the electronic mic voice Quinn herself had rigged up. "Will you please forgive us? *Pleeeease?*" the robot begged.

"Please?" Zoey added, appearing in the doorway with Logan, Chase, Michael, and Lola.

"Well, only because I love tulips," Quinn said, smiling at last.

Zoey and Lola hugged Quinn at the same time. Chase picked up the tulips and handed them to Quinn.

"Thanks," Quinn said, shyly looking down. "So, you guys fixed the Loganator." Quinn was impressed.

"Yeah," Chase said. It hadn't been easy. Quinn only made it look that way. The girl had a real gift. "Listen," Chase said seriously. "We're really sorry."

"All of you?" Quinn asked skeptically.

Slowly every set of eyes in the room settled on Logan. "Yes," he confirmed.

"Good." Quinn grinned, relieved. It was great to have her friends back. All of them. Except... "Hey, where's Nicole?" Quinn asked.

"Um, she has a date tonight," Zoey said, hoping that would be the end of the conversation.

"Who with?" Quinn asked.

It was a good question.

As the record spun on the player and the candles burned on the side table, Nicole slouched in her chair, wondering how she ever let Zoey talk her into this.

Her date might have been the smartest guy at PCA, but he had not stopped smiling that creepy smile at her since she arrived in his corner of the library. "You look ravishing under fluorescent lighting, do you know that, Nicole?" he asked.

Nicole looked up at the library's bank of fluorescent lights. "Okay," she said, not sure if she'd been paid a compliment or not. Her sparkling pink tank was twinkling nicely, but it looked a lot better in sunlight.

"Crudités?" Miles offered her a small platter of cut vegetables.

"Sure!" Nicole reached for a carrot but didn't get a finger on it before Miles snatched back the plate.

"Oh, drat, I forgot the dip!" he exclaimed. "A moment," he said, excusing himself.

When she was alone, Nicole clenched her teeth and smoothed her flowered turquoise skirt. She might have looked great under the lights, but inside she was seething. "Zoey, you are so dead," she said aloud.

Voice Activated

Quinn sat at Dean Rivers's desk, intently tightening a screw on the bottom of a newly invented contraption. The robot war victory was now a sweet memory, and she and her friends were back on track.

Across the large executive office, Dean Rivers stood waiting anxiously, his hands shoved deep in the pockets of his khaki pants. "Well, is it ready?" he asked, leaning forward a little to peer at Quinn's work.

"Patience, Dean Rivers," Quinn said, glancing over at him amusedly. Adults could be so impatient. The dean had been hovering over her since the minute she sat down and began to set up his new system. "I just have to adjust the auditory flux modulator."

Dean Rivers shrugged casually. "Of course," he agreed, looking a little perplexed.

Quinn grinned, knowing full well that he had no

idea what she was talking about. When it came to her inventions and experiments, few did. At least he knew enough to be excited.

She set her contraption down carefully on his desk. It looked a little like the controls for a video game, but with several colored buttons and two rabbit ears in the back. "There," she said with satisfaction. "Your auto-mated voice-activation system is ready to rock." She did a tiny little shimmy in the dean's fancy leather chair. Oh, yes. This was going to be good.

"Great!" Dean Rivers said excitedly. Then he stopped, unsure what to do next. He was like a little kid who had just opened a new toy he had no idea how to play with. "What do I do?" he asked.

Quinn grinned and got to her feet. "Say 'lights,'" she said proudly.

"Lights," Dean Rivers echoed.

In an instant the lights went out.

"Now say it again," Quinn instructed.

"Lights!" Dean Rivers said more confidently.

The lights came on again.

"Very cool!" Dean Rivers said.

"Yup." Quinn nodded, and the ends of her French-braided hair bobbed. It was very cool — and was about to get cooler. "Want some coffee?" she asked.

"Sure," Dean Rivers replied.

She raised an eyebrow at the dean. "Then say it."

"Coffee." Something beeped behind Dean Rivers, and the coffeemaker on the credenza started to percolate. The dean wheeled around and bent low to watch the rich brown drink drip into the pot. "I love this," he told Quinn earnestly.

"Who wouldn't?" Quinn asked. It was magic at your fingertips, or rather, your vocal cords. "Now . . . close the door."

"All right," Dean Rivers said agreeably. Without thinking, he started walking toward the door.

"Nope!" Quinn chortled, raising a finger in the air a little gleefully. She loved it when her inventions made life easier. "Don't do it, just say it."

Dean Rivers stopped in his tracks. "Door," he said. The door swung closed with a soft click. "Excellent," the dean declared.

With her job finished, Quinn walked back to the dean's desk and began to gather her tools. She put everything neatly back into her black leather doctor's-kit-like bag. Her work here was done . . . and perfectly.

With a final check for any forgotten materials, Quinn started for the door. She was halfway there when she remembered something. "Oh," she said, smiling mysteriously up at the dean. "And if your office is ever invaded by an intruder, just yell 'dogs.'" She whispered the last word quietly.

"Dogs?" Dean Rivers asked questioningly.

"Shhh!" Quinn scolded — the computer might hear him! "Only if you are in danger," she instructed.

Dean Rivers put a finger to his lips and nodded knowingly. "Right."

"Well, I'd better get to class," Quinn said with a small wave.

"Okay, well, thanks for getting me all hooked up," Dean Rivers said.

"I'll e-mail you my bill," Quinn added before flouncing out the door. *"Ciao!"*

Dean Rivers watched her go, then considered what voice command he should activate first. He was still deciding when his assistant buzzed him. "Dean Rivers, your wife is here to see you," she informed him.

A look of panic came over Dean Rivers's face. "My wife? Uh, tell her I'm not here." He knew it wouldn't get rid of her, but it would probably buy him a little time. He pushed a button on Quinn's contraption and quickly climbed under his desk. He was not anxious to see the Mrs. He had a feeling she was not very happy with him and his love of electronic toys.

"Mrs. Rivers! He's not in there!" The dean heard his assistant say in a loud voice.

"Don't give me that," Mrs. Rivers replied angrily as she burst into her husband's office. "Carl? Carl, what kind of grown man spends two thousand dollars on video games?" she demanded.

Fear and guilt made Dean Rivers shudder slightly under his desk. Then, quietly, he reached up and pulled Quinn's voice-activation machine down close to his face. "Dogs," he whispered into it.

A second later the sound of sirens and barking attack dogs filled the office. Mrs. Rivers looked around frantically to see where the noise was coming from. Unable to locate it she dashed out the door to safety.

Still under his desk, Dean Rivers let out a huge sigh of relief. Having a scientific genius on campus really paid off. "Thank you, Quinn," he whispered.

CHAPTER 8
Horse

Outside on the basketball court, Chase, Michael, and Logan were in the middle of a mean game of HORSE. Michael had the ball.

"All righty boys, check it out," he said cockily, adjusting his Stingrays T-shirt and dribbling the ball. It was his turn to call the shot. "Back to the basket, eyes closed" — he paused long enough to close his eyes with his own fingertips, — "reverse hook, off the backboard, and in."

"Oh, come on," Chase groaned. Nobody could make a basket that way. Michael may have been his best bud, but the dude could be a total showboat — especially when a certain girl was nearby.

"Relax," Logan assured Chase, crossing his arms over his signature black tank. "That shot's impossible."

"Oh, is it?" Michael asked, turning around briefly

to raise an eyebrow at his roommates. He dribbled the ball twice and threw it with one hand over his head toward the basket. It hit the backboard dead center and slipped into the net. *Swish!*

"Oh, ah-ha-ha-ha," Michael gloated. "Did someone say *impossible*?" he said, stretching out his ear and glancing over his shoulder to see if Vanessa was still watching their game. She'd been hanging out with a couple of friends nearby since the game started.

"Yeah, you keep showing off for Vanessa," Logan announced, cradling the ball under his arm.

"Oh, is that Vanessa over there?" Michael asked, all innocence. As if he hadn't noticed!

"Dude, why don't you just ask her out?" Chase wanted to know. Michael was clearly crazy about her.

Michael balked. He wanted to, he really did. But Vanessa was so . . . so . . . "Nah, she's too cute," he said, a little embarrassed. "I'd throw up."

"Ah, girls love that," Logan said with mock seriousness, giving Michael a pitying jab on the shoulder. Some guys really struggled with the opposite sex. Logan was glad he was not one of them.

"Yeah, just puke on her and you're in like Flynn." Chase pointed at Michael with both hands. Maybe he should try that move. Or NOT.

"Hey, can we just get back to the game?" Michael asked, swiping the ball from Logan and thrusting it at Chase. He gave his friend a little push toward the throw line. Anything to change the subject — just talking about Vanessa made him a little queasy.

"You're up, dog," Michael told his curly-headed friend.

Chase dribbled the ball, thinking about how he was going to make Michael's crazy shot.

"Score?" Logan inquired. All that talk about girls had made his mind wander from the game.

"Uh, I got H," Michael reported proudly. "You have *H-O*, and Chase has *H-O-R*."

Chase turned around long enough to give Michael the evil eye. "Yes, I'm losing," he agreed grimly. "We're all clear on that." He closed his eyes, took a second to focus, and tossed the ball over his head toward the basket. It didn't even go close to the net.

"Oh, and he gets the *S*," Michael called out as he caught the ball and slung it low on his hip.

Chase turned grumpily. It was one thing to lose. It was another to be taunted about it. "No," he said, shaking his head. "I reject the *S*."

"You missed," Logan reminded him, stepping closer. "You can't reject the *S*."

Sure he could. Yes, he missed. Yes, he was still losing, but nobody could make him take the S. "I hate S," Chase announced. "I'm starting a petition to remove S from the alphabet."

Michael shook his head sadly. "Dude, you can't live without S." It was practically the most popular letter!

"I could live the rest of my life without ever using a word that has an S in it," Chase insisted, folding his arms over his purple PCA tee.

"I bet I could go longer than you," Logan challenged. If Chase didn't need S, then neither did he.

"Shall we make this a three-way bet?" Michael inquired, cocking his head and eyeing his roommates.

"Bring it," Chase said in a taunting voice, wagging his fingers in the air.

"Okay," Michael said, still thinking. If this was a three-way challenge, and it looked like it was, he wanted to make the stakes good. "The first one of us who uses a word with the letter S in it has to . . ." The perfect idea hadn't come to him yet. Then it did. "Run through campus wearing nothing but a bikini top and a hula skirt."

"And with a flashing light on his head," Chase added, gesturing to his own wild curls.

Logan eyed his friends warily, glad that he

wouldn't be the loser. How stupid did these dudes want to look? Logan actually felt a little sorry for them. But if they wanted to look like idiots, that was their problem. . . . "It's a bet," he said before they could change their minds. He was going to enjoy this.

"I'm in," Michael said.

The three guys linked their hands together in a cross shake.

"Okay," Chase said. "S's are off-limits starting . . . now." He raised his arms in the air and pointed to the ground. They were off.

"Okay," Michael agreed, suddenly completely aware of every word he said. He'd have to talk pretty slowly to make sure he didn't slip an accidental S into any of his sentences. "Do you people want to continue playing the game that we were recently playing?" he inquired. Nice. Not a single S.

"Ye —" Logan caught himself just in time. "Indeed," he corrected. "I would like to continue playing that game."

"Well," Chase began. "I am hungry . . . and would like to go get a tuna fi — food item." Whew. He'd almost said *fish* and *sandwich*. This might be trickier than he'd thought. "To eat."

"Hey, here comes . . . the girl you like," Logan said haltingly as Vanessa walked by with a couple of her friends.

"Right. Girl very pretty," Chase commented, tilting his head to watch Vanessa walk by.

Michael rubbed his hands together nervously. "Correct," he agreed. Vanessa was undeniably beautiful.

Vanessa stopped and looked their way. "Hi, Michael," she said, flashing him a warm smile.

"Hey, Vane —" He couldn't say her name, or he'd lose the bet! But there she was, standing right in front of him, and she'd just said hello! He laughed to avoid saying the rest of her name. "Hey, you," he finally greeted. Oh, man! That was totally, completely lame.

Vanessa and her friends looked at Michael like he was demented, then strode off in a pack.

CHAPTER 9

Family Emergency

Across campus in the girls' lounge, Zoey, Nicole, and Lola were crowded around a computer screen. They were looking up all kinds of random stuff — you could find it all on the Internet!

"See, I told you," Zoey said, glancing down at her mint-green tank with the watermelon-colored bridge motif. It was perfect for this warm spring day. "One regular bagel, three hundred calories."

"How many carbs?" Nicole asked.

"Nobody counts carbs anymore," Zoey replied. Sometimes Nicole could be a little slow.

"Yeah," Lola agreed, realizing for the first time that carb counting was over. "When did people stop counting carbs?"

Zoey shrugged. She'd never been a carb counter

and was glad the fad was finished. "When they figured out it was stupid," she said with a smile.

Lola nodded and her tiny hot-pink ponytail extension — the one that matched her black-and-pink embellished T-shirt — swayed slightly. Zoey had a point.

Zoey grabbed the computer mouse, ready for the next search. But before she could type in anything else, Quinn came barging into the room on her phone.

"I know, just sign on right now," she said into the small silver device. She snapped her phone shut and elbowed Lola out of the seat in front of the computer. "Get off the computer. I need it," she ordered.

Lola backed off, but not without a glare. What was with the attitude? "Why can't you use the computer in your room?" she asked pointedly. She didn't mind sharing, but Quinn didn't have to be so rude. . . .

"The wireless is down," Quinn reported matter-of-factly. "Now hush. There's an illness in my family." She clicked the mouse a couple of times and stared intently at the screen. "Otis," she called a little frantically, her eyebrows knit together. "Otis, can you hear me?" She adjusted her square-framed glasses and squinted at the screen. "Look into the camera!" she urged anxiously.

Zoey, Lola, and Nicole exchanged concerned looks.

Then a strange sound came through the computer speakers. It was kind of a bleat, kind of a roar. And it sounded . . . sad.

Zoey stared at the screen, surprised. She had been expecting to see a sick person. "Is that a llama?" she asked, leaning in closer for a better look.

"Otis is not a llama," Quinn said defensively. "He's an alpaca."

And the difference was? Zoey held up her hands innocently. She didn't mean to offend anyone, especially when something was clearly wrong. "Sorry," she mumbled.

"I got him for Christmas when I was nine, and he's my very best friend in the world," Quinn explained, never taking her eyes off the screen.

"So, what's wrong with him?" Lola asked, trying to be extra sensitive. Having an alpaca for a pet was weird, but whatever. Quinn was really upset.

"I'm not sure," Quinn admitted sadly. "He's been sick for three weeks. The veterinarian is there right now talking with my parents."

"Hi, Quinny," a perky, red-haired woman in a sea-green T-shirt greeted the girl, waving wildly. "Can you see me on the computer? Look —" She pointed to her face excitedly. "I got my eyebrows waxed!"

"That's great, Mom," Quinn said dismissively. Her mom never was very good at focusing on the issue at hand. "Dad, is the vet there?" she asked, hoping he had a better handle on things.

"Yes, she's right here!" Quinn's father yelled, as if Quinn were deaf, or the computer connection was really two cans and a string. He was not as flighty as her mom, but her dad was no mechanical genius. Quinn often wondered where she got her smarts. . . . "Dr. Lang!" her dad beckoned the vet. Then while he waited for the animal doctor, he ran forward and zoomed the camera in on Otis. The sick alpaca had a shaggy, caramel-colored mane around his head, liquid-brown eyes, and a whitish face.

Otis let out another mournful bellow.

A dark-haired woman in a white lab coat stuck her face in close to Otis's. "Hello, Quinn," she greeted the girl on the other end. "I'm Doctor Lang."

Zoey stared at the vet. She looked a lot like . . . Quinn, right down to her long dark hair and square glasses frames.

"So what's wrong with Otis?" Quinn asked, getting right to the point. "Why has he been crying and not eating?"

"Well, I can't be sure," Dr. Lang admitted. "But my

best guess is that Otis is, well, depressed." She gave the forlorn alpaca a pet.

Quinn's heart sank. Her baby! Depressed!

"A depressed llama?" Nicole muttered, eyeing the screen skeptically. That was even stranger than having a llama for a pet in the first place!

"Alpaca! Now hush!" Quinn scolded. The look on her face alone was enough to silence Nicole.

"Why would Otis be depressed?" Quinn asked worriedly. Then a terrible thought entered her mind. "Mom, have you been reading him your romance novels again?" she questioned.

Quinn's mother leaned into view. "No baby!" she vowed, gently stroking a newly waxed eyebrow.

Well, that was good. But if it wasn't bad romances, it could only be . . .

"Quinn, I think he's depressed because he misses you," Dr. Lang said.

Quinn felt a sharp pang of guilt. She knew it! She'd gone off on a great new adventure, discovered new things, and made new friends. Otis was left behind with . . . her parents! "Oh, I'm a terrible, terrible person," Quinn moaned. "Oh, Otis, I never should have left you to come to PCA."

"It's okay," Nicole said cheerfully. "People get

over depression. My uncle Rodney was depressed for years."

"How did he get better?" Quinn asked. Maybe there was hope for her four-legged furry friend.

"He didn't," Nicole admitted, looking down at her cobalt-blue tank with taupe embroidery across the top. "He robbed a convenience store and got arrested." She shook her head sadly. Poor Uncle Rodney.

Zoey rolled her eyes and leaned in close to Nicole. "Why would you tell that story?" she asked. Was that supposed to cheer Quinn up? I mean, really. She loved Nicole, but sometimes the girl said amazingly stupid things.

"Quinn, is there any way you could come home for a few days?" Dr. Lang asked. "I think Otis would be fine if he could just spend a couple of days with you."

Quinn's face brightened. Of course, she just needed to go home. Immediately.

"You can't go home," Lola pointed out. "It's the middle of the semester."

Right. The dean would never allow it. Quinn's heart was beginning to sink again when her mother reappeared on screen next to Otis. "Don't worry, sweetie, we'll cheer up your ostrich," she crooned.

Quinn's heart plummeted down to her feet. "Mom,

he's an alpaca!" she shouted. Couldn't anybody get that right?

"Love you, too, sweetie!" her mom said with a wave.

Quinn stared at the screen as it went black. The words CONNECTION TERMINATED flashed across it in red. Her mother acted as if nothing was the matter! Quinn hung her head, consumed with sadness and guilt.

Zoey reached out a hand. "Aw, Quinn, now don't you go getting all depressed," she coaxed.

"I'm not depressed," Quinn replied in a monotone. She looked a little like Otis.

Zoey, Lola, and Nicole exchanged concerned looks. This was not good.

A couple of days later the girls spotted Quinn playing the trombone under an old oak tree. The notes she played were painful — awkward and moaning — just like Otis's bellows.

Even from thirty yards away, the music made Zoey wince. "She is so depressed," she told Lola and Nicole.

"Yeah," Lola agreed, shaking her head and making her giant shell earrings jangle. That was not music. "Listen to that." Actually, she would have preferred not to. In fact, she had to force herself not to shove her fingers in her ears.

Zoey watched Quinn, feeling terrible. The girl was seriously hurting. "I've never seen Quinn like this," she said. Except for the time she and the gang accidentally hurt Quinn's feelings, she was always cheerful and busy with her experiments. Zoey hadn't seen her with a test tube or an electrical wire in her hands in days. It just wasn't normal . . . normal for Quinn, anyway. "We should do something for her."

"Hey!" Zoey said, getting a great idea. She shook her layered blond hair over the shoulders of her peachy paisley print tee. "We should throw her, like, a really cool party."

A party? Lola thought for a minute. It was an interesting idea, but . . . "Her birthday was three months ago," she pointed out.

"Not a birthday party," Zoey said. Duh. Of course she knew when Quinn's birthday was.

"What, you mean like an alpaca party?" Lola asked, eyeing Zoey. She was all for cheering Quinn up, but could there be a weirder theme?

She turned to Nicole for reinforcement. Nicole looked great in her sleeveless light purple top, but her face was all scrunched up. Yup, even Nicole knew throwing a wacky llama party was a crazy idea.

"Yeah," Zoey said. She knew it was weird, but who cared? The important thing was cheering Quinn up. "Like a whole alpaca theme." Yeah, an alpaca party might just do the trick. . . .

"All right," Nicole said with a nod. Zoey was sure, and that was enough for her. She was game for anything, especially if it would put an end to this awful music! "When should we do it?" Nicole asked.

Just then Quinn hit a particularly bad, particularly loud note.

"As soon as possible," Zoey declared.

CHAPTER 10

Don't Say It!

Chase, Michael, and Logan sat in the back of history class listening to their teacher drone on about the Boston Tea Party. Bo-ring.

"On the evening of September the sixteenth, seventeen seventy-four, thousands of Bostonians packed into the old south meeting house to hear Samuel Adams speak," the teacher said excitedly before turning to the board.

As soon as his back was to the students, Michael leaned in toward his friends. "You . . . two people . . . are going to loo —" Oops. He couldn't say that. "Not win the bet," he finished. Nice save, if he did say so himself.

"No," Logan piped up. "You will" — he paused, searching for a synonym for lose — "not win, for I can go longer without" — pause — "invoking the letter after R." Wow, impressive. He'd just used the word *invoking*.

This no-S thing was good for his vocabulary if nothing else.

Chase shook his head. "I will win the bet, for one of you will . . . talk the bad letter before me do." He made a face at his bad grammar, which was even more glaring than his bright yellow T-shirt. "Before me," he corrected. "No need for the *do*." Man, this was getting kind of tedious.

"Chase, Michael, Logan," the teacher called out from the front of the room. He had a major scowl on his face. "You guys have been whispering for the entire class."

Busted. Chase looked sheepishly at his teacher. "I apologize," he said honestly.

Logan pointed a pencil at Chase victoriously. "Ha!" he cried. He'd heard the soothing "S" sound he'd been waiting for!

Chase shot him a look. *"Z,"* he said. Apparently Logan could not spell.

Logan's face fell. "Oh, right," he said, disappointed. He had been looking forward to seeing Chase in a grass skirt. And he knew that he would eventually. No way Chase could hold out for much longer. All Logan had to do was wait . . . and if Chase didn't blow it, Michael was bound to!

Alpaca Party

In Brenner Hall, the girls were getting ready to throw Quinn the best alpaca party ever. The room was decorated with streamers of every size, shape, and color. They hung from the ceiling, the walls — even some of the furniture.

Lola strolled into the room carrying a giant cake. "Guys, check out the alpaca cake," she said proudly as she set it on one of the small round tables.

"Whoa, it's perfect," Zoey congratulated her. It looked just like a little alpaca, and totally delicious.

Lola nodded knowingly. Of course it was. She knew how to get the job done. Even when it was as weird as this.

Nicole immediately snuck a finger to the edge of the cake. She hoped the cute cake was not alpaca flavored. She was starving, and the creamy yellow icing looked so fluffy and sweet. . . .

Whack! Zoey slapped her friend's hand lightly and she recoiled. "Not until Quinn sees it," she scolded Nicole. Who was this party for, anyway? And it wouldn't be long now. They had everything ready. Or almost everything . . .

"Hey, where's the alpaca costume?" Lola asked, glancing at Nicole. The costume was Nicole's job.

"Oh, yeah, where is it?" Zoey echoed.

Nicole looked at her friends a little sheepishly. She'd been kind of hoping they'd forget about the alpaca costume altogether. . . . "Uh, Mark," she called nervously. "Come over here."

A giant blue figure with a very l-o-n-g nose ambled into the lounge. Nicole tried not to wince as the awful blue beast came closer.

"Uh, that's an aardvark," Lola said in a total "duh" voice.

Nicole tried not to feel like a complete idiot. She'd known the costume was all wrong, but after searching and searching, it was the best she could do. At least it started with an *a*. "Well, you try finding an alpaca costume," she blurted miserably. "They don't exist!"

Suddenly the aardvark reached his furry blue arms up and lifted off his giant head. Underneath, Mark Del Figgalo's real head was drenched with sweat and he was panting hard.

"Ewww," Lola remarked, poking gingerly at Mark's damp hair. "Why are you all sweaty?"

"It's a million degrees in here," Mark whimpered as he gasped for air. "Do I have to wear the head?" He and Quinn had been dating for a while, and he would do almost anything for her, but this was giving him flashbacks to the time at Halloween when he was glued inside a mummy costume. And he thought his brain might be cooking.

"Yes!" the girls chorused together. There was no question in Zoey's mind. Anything that might cheer up their friend was worth the effort.

Overruled, Mark reluctantly put the aardvark head back on.

Just then a trio of girls hurried into the lounge. "Hey, guys," they called excitedly. "Quinn's coming!"

Everyone crowded over to one side of the lounge, behind the alpaca cake. One of the girls even held a small stuffed alpaca. Everyone was ready.

"Hit the music," Zoey said. Someone pressed a button on the multicolored CD player, and a popular pop song played through the speakers. A moment later Quinn walked into the room wearing an earth-tone shirt. Zoey thought she might be dressing in solidarity with Otis. She hadn't worn any of her usual funky-colored cheerful clothing in days. Her hair was pulled back tightly — no braids or feathers — and her expression was glum.

"Surprise!" everyone shouted and clapped.

"What's all this?" Quinn asked, clearly surprised.

"It's an alpaca party," Zoey explained.

Nicole blew a little party horn.

"Moooo!" Mark's muffled voice called out from under his blue aardvark head. Some of the girls turned to glare at him. Alpacas did not moo!

"An alpaca party?" Quinn asked. She seemed a little taken aback. "Why?"

"To cheer you up," Nicole explained. Uh, why else would anyone throw an alpaca party?

"'Cause we know how much you miss Otis," Zoey added gently.

"You guys are so sweet," Quinn said, smiling for the first time in days.

"Well, it gets better," Zoey said a little mysteriously. "Turn it on."

A big screen on the wall came to life and Otis's

fuzzy face appeared, flanked by Quinn's parents. All three of them were decked out in party hats.

"Otis!" Quinn cried gleefully, stepping up to the screen. It always made her feel so great to see him.

Otis bellowed mournfully.

"Look, Quinn," her mother called. "We're on the Interweb again!"

"Happy alpaca party, baby," her father said with a giant wave.

"Thanks, Dad," Quinn replied, feeling her heart swell with joy. "Oh, Otis, you look so cute with your party hat on."

Otis bellowed again, and Quinn peered closely at his fuzzy alpaca face. Beneath his bright party wear he looked gloomy. "He still seems depressed," she said, her heart sinking again.

Zoey watched her friend slump down on the sofa arm. She had to distract her, fast!

"Come on, Quinn, let's cut the cake!" she encouraged cheerfully.

"Yeah, the cake!" the girls echoed.

Quinn stood up. "First I gotta go get my camera to take pictures of all this."

"Well, okay," Nicole agreed. "But hurry back,

'cause, you know, cake." Her tummy rumbled as she eyed the beautiful yellow frosting. It was calling to her.

"I'll hurry," Quinn replied solemnly. "I promise."

The girls watched her leave. "Think we made her happy?" Lola asked.

"I think so," Zoey replied, trying to sound convincing. It was hard to tell.

"Can I take my head off now?" Mark asked through his mask.

"No!" the girls replied in unison.

Dejected, the aardvark turned and headed back into a corner.

An hour later the girls were still sitting around the lounge waiting for Quinn to come back with her camera. The CD player was on its third disc!

"Where is she?" Lola asked, checking her watch with a yawn. She was lying on the retro-print polka-dot couch across from Zoey. She'd been sitting there so long that the French blue halter dress and long string of colored beads she'd donned for the party didn't even look fabulous anymore.

"How long can it take to get a camera?" Nicole added, leaning over the back of the couch droopily.

Her party mood had completely vanished, and her stomach had probably shrunk from waiting so long. If she had to go any longer, she was going to eat the decorations!

"I better go check on her," Zoey said, getting to her feet.

As soon as she disappeared out the door, Mark pulled the aardvark head off. "Okay," he panted. "It's, like, a hundred and twenty degrees in this thing. I can't keep this head on!"

Nicole and Lola turned and glared. Their looks said it all. With a giant sigh, Mark pulled the head back on yet again.

Nicole was just settling in for more waiting when Zoey came through the door, reading a piece of paper. "Where's Quinn?" Nicole asked.

Zoey looked up from the note, her expression full of worry. "She ran away," she said, trying to sound calm. This was serious.

CHAPTER 12
Search Party

The girls crowded around Zoey to try to make sense of Quinn's note.

"Okay, how do we know that Quinn ran away?" Nicole asked reasonably.

"Yeah, what does her note say exactly?" Lola added.

"'I'm running away,'" Zoey read from the paper in her hand. "Which to me sounds like she's running away." She didn't want to be sarcastic but she was feeling frustrated. Why didn't her friends believe her? And more important, why hadn't Quinn talked to them before doing something so rash?

"Did she say why?" someone from the party crowd asked.

"Yeah," Zoey replied. "She said she has to go home to be with Otis in his time of need."

Nicole sighed a little dreamily. "A girl and her beast," she said. It was almost like the movies!

A muffled voice came from the fuzzy blue creature behind them. "So hot . . ." Mark mumbled deep in the aardvark costume. "And dizzy . . ."

Lola ignored it. "I guess our alpaca party just made Quinn miss Otis even more," she said thoughtfully, taking a sip of her Blix.

"Hey," Nicole suddenly said, leaning forward. "If she leaves the PCA campus without permission, can't she get suspended?"

"Or worse," another girl added gravely.

"We gotta stop her!" Zoey said, getting to her feet. Depression *and* suspension? It would be too much for Quinn to handle.

"And fast," Lola added, checking her black-and-white checkered watch. "It's gonna be dark soon."

"Okay," Zoey agreed. "But we need to split up so we can cover more of the campus faster."

"Right." The rest of the girls all nodded in agreement as they got to their feet and followed Zoey out the door.

The party was over. Only the fuzzy blue beast was left in the lounge. He staggered around, then pulled off the giant aardvark head. Air . . . he just needed some air. Only it wasn't enough. All that time in the hot mask had made him weak. Mark swayed a bit, then fell over . . . *splat!* Right into the alpaca cake.

Outside, the students searched all over for Quinn. Nicole led a small pack of girls up a flight of stairs, while Lola and some friends split up near a fountain. Zoey was scouring the parking lot in case Quinn had called a cab. "Quinn?" she yelled. "Quinn, where are you?"

Then she spotted her — lugging a rolling suitcase up a flight of stairs. "Quinn!" she called, relieved to see her still on school grounds. She'd found her in time.

"Don't try to stop me," Quinn said angrily. She was sick of being here, just waiting. Nothing was going to keep her from Otis!

"You can't leave PCA," Zoey insisted. She knew she had to be careful not to make Quinn even more upset. But she couldn't let her get into trouble!

"Otis needs me!" Quinn shouted down the stairs as she lugged her suitcase ever upward. The big bag weighed a ton, thanks to all of the lab equipment inside.

Zoey followed her up the stairs, finally catching up to her at the top. She grabbed Quinn by the arm and whirled her around.

"Leave me alone!" Quinn hissed.

"No!" Zoey said flatly. She wasn't about to let Quinn throw away her PCA experience. The girl loved it here!

"What do you want?" Quinn asked desperately.

"I'm not letting you leave PCA," Zoey told her. "You'll get suspended."

Quinn knew Zoey was right, but she had to take the risk. "There's a four-foot-tall furry bundle of sadness who needs me," she wailed, feeling consumed by helplessness. It was the worst feeling in the world.

"So what are you gonna do, Quinn?" Zoey challenged. "How are you gonna get home?"

"I don't know, monorail?" Quinn said, uttering the first crazy idea that came into her head.

"There's no monorail from California to Seattle," Zoey pointed out.

"Well, there should be!" Quinn yelled.

"Quinn." Zoey was getting exasperated now. Why couldn't the girl see that leaving without permission would be a huge mistake?

"I have to see Otis," Quinn said plainly, trying to make Zoey understand. She had no choice.

"Okay, look, just gimme time to think," Zoey said, sensing Quinn's seriousness and frustration. There had to be a better solution ... she only needed to find it. "Just let me try to fix this."

"How?" Quinn wanted to know.

"I don't know yet," Zoey admitted. "But you have to promise me you won't leave PCA."

Quinn stared at her friend. Zoey was no rocket scientist, but she could usually fix things. She had good ideas and good judgment. Quinn sighed. Maybe leaving PCA without permission wasn't such a smart plan — even if Otis did need her.

"All right," Quinn finally said, picking up her purple backpack and slinging it over her shoulder.

"All right?" Zoey asked, just to be sure.

"All right," Quinn repeated as she started back down the stairs, dragging her suitcase behind her. She just hoped Otis would be all right, too.

CHAPTER 13

Game Over?

The next day Lola and Nicole were having lunch with Chase and Michael at one of the outdoor café tables. While they ate, the girls were filling the guys in on the crazy stuff that had been going on with Quinn.

"Quinn actually tried to leave PCA?" Chase said haltingly. He still had to speak pretty slowly to make sure he didn't mistakenly slip an *S* in anywhere.

"To go be . . . with her alpaca?" Michael asked in an equally stilted voice. Being on *S* alert 24/7 required keen attention. Luckily he was up to the task.

Only Lola was not. "Okay," Lola said, letting go of her chunky orange-and-lime-colored beads and interrupting the guys. "How long is this going to go on?" Their silly bet about not using the letter *S*, and the slow convoluted way it made them talk, was starting to drive her crazy.

"Yeah, would one of you just use a word with the letter S in it already so we can have a normal conversation?" Nicole suggested. Talking to the guys right now was worse than talking to the guys back home.

"No. I am determined . . . to go longer than Michael and Logan without uttering . . . that letter," Chase said haltingly. He sounded like a malfunctioning robot — even to himself.

Lola rolled her eyes. These boys were going to drive her insane! "Ugh. Could this be more annoying?" she asked Nicole.

"No!" Nicole practically shouted. The boys were so irritating that it was bringing her down — and on the day she had worn her new jade-green tee with the princess sleeves! Grabbing her Blix, Nicole took a frustrated sip.

"Michael," Chase said, nodding over the edge of the patio to the level below. "There be the girl you like."

"Michael likes her?" Lola asked, turning around to get a good look. Who was this girl?

Michael nodded. There was no use denying his crush on Vanessa. It was out of his control.

"What's her name?" Lola inquired. Maybe now they could have a normal conversation.

"Tell her, Michael," Chase suggested with a smirk. "Tell her the name of the girl you . . . enjoy."

Michael rolled his eyes. Did Chase think he was stupid enough to fall for that? He'd successfully avoided the letter *S* for days! "Nice try," he said. "But I will not do that."

"Her name must have an *S* in it," Nicole said resignedly. She might as well get used to this ridiculousness. Or else go buy some earplugs . . .

"Give me your cell phone," Lola said to Nicole, picking it up off the table before the girl could answer. She had an idea.

"What're you gonna do?" Nicole asked. She had better not use up her minutes!

Lola flipped open the phone. "I'm gonna trick Logan into losing so we don't have to listen to these guys talk like idiots anymore."

Nicole smiled. That sounded like a great plan. Lola could talk all she wanted if she could end this bet!

"Hey," Michael objected. He turned his wounded eyes on Chase. "Lola called we the plural of idiot."

"I am offended," Chase said with a pout.

Lola ignored the guys altogether. She was busy executing her brilliant plan. "Logan's last name is Reese, with an *S*, right?" Lola looked to Nicole for confirmation.

"Yeah," Nicole said. She could tell the girl was scheming seriously, but wasn't sure where she was going with her plan.

"Good," Lola said with a small smile. She looked over the edge of the patio to where Logan was sitting with some of his friends below and dialed his number. Logan picked it up on the third ring.

"Lo for Logan," Logan greeted.

"Hiiii," Lola said in a sultry grown-up voice. "This is Jammin' Jean from KP-one-oh-seven, and you've just won a trip for two to Honolulu!"

"No way, for real?" Logan asked. Not that he was all that surprised. Luck pretty much followed him around.

"For real," Lola continued in her DJ voice. "Now, all you gotta do is tell us your name." Lola grinned at Nicole, who smiled back excitedly. Not long now.

"Logan," Logan replied quickly.

"And your last name?" Lola asked.

"Ree . . ." Logan caught himself just in time.

"Reee . . . what?" Lola was not going to give up easily. The sooner this stupid bet was over, the better. Way better.

Logan pulled the phone away from his ear and looked around. This had to be a prank.

"Come on, for the love of godfrey, what?" Lola was trying to keep her sultry DJ voice. It wasn't easy. She was just one simple word away from ending the torture!

Finally Logan looked up and saw Lola, Nicole, and his roommates at a table on the balcony. And little Miss Lola was on the phone. "Re . . . jected!" Logan crowed, thrusting a finger in the air toward their table. "Buh-bye." He snapped his phone shut gleefully.

Ugh! Lola closed Nicole's phone with a heavy sigh. So close, and yet so far.

CHAPTER
14
All Bets Off

Zoey knocked lightly on Dean Rivers's door. The lights in his office were flashing on and off, and she could see the dean sitting at his desk talking frantically into some kind of electronic contraption. "Lights, lights," he cried repeatedly.

Suddenly the sound of barking dogs echoed through the room. "I didn't say 'dogs'!" the dean bellowed. "Hey!" he shouted to no one in particular. He rammed a finger over several buttons, to no avail. Lights flashed, dogs barked, sirens screamed — and in no particular order. "Beverly, did you reach Quinn?" he yelled to his assistant.

Zoey was pretty sure Beverly wouldn't be able to hear him or her over the din. She knocked again, a lot louder this time. "Dean Rivers, you got a sec?" she asked loudly.

"No!" he practically shouted, still pushing buttons. Then he waved a hand. "Yes, come in."

Zoey stepped gingerly into the office. She didn't think there were any attack dogs in there, but with all the barking you could never be too sure . . .

"Keep trying to get Quinn here!" the dean shouted to his assistant. He adjusted the rabbit ears on the electronic contraption and pushed a few more buttons. Nothing. He looked up at Zoey, an exhausted expression on his face. "Life is hard," he murmured.

A moment later Beverly came into the office carrying a document attached to a clipboard. "Dean Rivers, can I get you to sign this please?" she asked.

"I suppose," the dean replied forlornly.

Zoey tried not to smile. The dean was clearly at his wits' end, which would definitely work in her favor. "What's up with the lights?" Zoey asked. The dogs seemed to have stopped barking — for a second, anyway.

"Oh, Quinn set up this voice-control system and I spilled coffee on this thing here and now it's all ker-plooey." The dean stared at the control panel and sighed. "Watch."

Leaning forward, the dean spoke a single word into the contraption. "Lights."

Behind Zoey, the office door slammed shut, just as Beverly was about to walk through it. *Wham!* She crashed right into the hard wood, smashing her face.

"Owwww, my nose!" she cried, covering her face with her free hand.

"Yeah, you should put some ice on that," the dean advised distractedly. He was still fiddling with Quinn's malfunctioning control panel.

"Thank you, sir," Beverly replied, still holding her nose.

"I called Quinn five times and she refuses to come fix it. She says she's too depressed," Dean Rivers told Zoey hopelessly.

"Well, that's actually what I came to talk to you about," Zoey said, raising an eyebrow. It looked like Dean Rivers might just be desperate enough to accept her proposal. "I think I know how we can cheer her up."

The dean dropped the control and looked up at Zoey, all ears. "How?" he asked.

"Have you ever heard of an alpaca?" Zoey asked.

"Alpaca?" the dean echoed, his bushy eyebrows knitting together. The sound of snarling attack dogs filled the air.

*   *   *

Across campus, Logan, Chase, and Michael were walking to class.

"Can you two believe?" Chase said carefully. No matter how long he went without saying it, the letter S was hard to avoid. "Half a week without the letter?"

"I can go much longer than that," Logan said haughtily. "Without . . . the letter." Sometimes having a limited vocabulary was a good thing. At least it kept Michael and Chase quieter.

"But I will go even longer . . . without it . . . for I will not be the one to wear that bikini top and hula bottom," Michael insisted.

"Don't forget the light on your head," Chase said, pointing to Michael's close-cropped afro.

"Your head," Michael shot back.

"No," Chase insisted. "For I will not be defeated."

"Nor will I," Logan added.

"Well, I think that you —"

Suddenly there was a voice behind him. A sweet voice. "Okay, Michael?" it said.

Michael whirled around. The sweet voice was Vanessa's, and she was standing right in front of him. And she looked . . . mad.

"Okay, Michael? I've been waiting six weeks for you to ask me out. What's up?" She folded her arms over her tangerine-colored shrug.

Michael stared at her, openmouthed. "Huh?" was all he could mutter. Vanessa was actually talking to him!

"Do you want to go out with me?" the girl asked plainly.

Michael sputtered and gestured wildly with his hands. Did he? Did he ever! But did he want to enough to say . . . "Yes!" he blurted. "I do!"

Chase eyed his friend. "*Yes* ends in *S*," he chortled.

"You lost, dude," Logan chided with an "I knew it wouldn't be me" nod.

What were they, kidding? The most beautiful girl on campus had just asked him out. Who cared about a stupid bet? "I don't care!" Michael hooted. "See? I will be escorting Miss Vanessa to Sushi Rox, okay? Yeah. And afterwards, perhaps we shall share a sorbet or soda." He enunciated each S with an emphatic flare. It felt great to use that letter again! "So . . . see ya!" He strolled over to Vanessa and took her arm. "Vanessa?" he intoned. The most beautiful S was in her name, of course. . . .

Chase and Logan watched them go.

"Sassy," Chase said, raising an eyebrow. If he had a date with the girl of his dreams, he wouldn't care about a bet, either. "That's three *S*'s," he added for Logan's benefit.

"Sweet," Logan said, slapping Chase an easy five. *S* was back.

CHAPTER 15

Alpaca Reunion

Zoey led Quinn across a big field at the edge of campus. She was trying not to smile, but it was hard. Quinn was going to be so excited!

But she wasn't . . . yet. "Zoey, where are you taking me?" Quinn grumbled as Zoey dragged her along. If she could not be with her beloved Otis, then she just wanted to stay holed up in her room . . . forever.

"Come on, talk less, walk more," Zoey coaxed, hiding her excitement. It was going to be good to have normal, er, the old Quinn back.

"I don't want to do anything fun," Quinn protested. "I told you, I'm too depressed about Otis to . . ."

Quinn broke off just as Zoey stopped in her tracks and looked up ahead toward the big oak tree. There, coming around the giant tree trunk, were Lola, Nicole, and . . .

"No, you did not!" Quinn said breathlessly, not believing her eyes. "Otis!" she screamed. She raced up to the alpaca and threw her arms around his neck. Otis bleated happily.

Zoey, Lola, and Nicole watched happily as Quinn petted and smooched her furry alpaca. "How did you get him to PCA?" Quinn asked, stroking Otis's fuzzy ears.

"Well . . ." Nicole began, trying not to worry about all the hair that had to be attaching itself to Quinn's cute lime-green top with the embroidered flowers. "Zoey called your mom," she finally managed to say.

"Who's a little insane," Lola put in. "So then Zoey asked to speak to your dad."

"And then we just set it up," Zoey finished. No need to go into details. The important thing was how wonderful it was to see Quinn smile again.

"Oh my gosh, this is so great!" Quinn squealed, wrapping her arms around Otis yet again. Then she stood up straight, frowning. "Oh, but we have to hide him. PCA has a strict rule against pets on campus." Quinn looked genuinely worried.

"It's cool, you're covered," Lola said. Her long, red halter blew around the tops of her legs.

"Dean Rivers said it's okay," Zoey confirmed. She still couldn't stop smiling. "But just for the weekend," she added. She needed Quinn to know that this arrangement wasn't permanent.

"As long as you fix his voice-control-system thingy," Nicole said, adjusting the yellow shrug she wore over her yellow T-shirt.

"No problem!" Quinn squealed. "Otis, did you hear that? We get to spend an entire weekend together!"

Otis made happy alpaca noises, and Quinn leaned over his neck and crooned the same sounds right back to him.

"Quinn speaks alpaca?" Nicole asked. She was so amazed that she forgot all about the hair.

Zoey shrugged. Of course she did. After all, they were talking about Quinn. "Are you surprised?"

"Come on, Otis, we're going to have the best weekend ever!" Quinn squealed. She was practically bouncing as she led him away.

Zoey smiled as she watched them walk back toward the campus buildings. Her plan had worked.

Quinn's fabulous weekend with Otis started immediately. She wanted him to see and do all of the things that she did at PCA — so he would understand why she had to be so far away from him.

First she paraded him proudly through campus,

giving him the grand tour. She waved at fellow students, friends, and faculty as they passed. Some smiled and waved back, but most of them stopped and stared, their mouths hanging open. Quinn didn't care. She and Otis were together, and that was all that mattered!

Later that afternoon they stopped for ice cream — vanilla for her and strawberry for Otis. The pair licked and munched to their hearts' content. Otis's big lips smushed the ice cream and broke up the cone in three seconds flat.

After their treat Quinn set up a little table on one of the quads and taught Otis how to play chess. After all, if he was going to hang out at PCA, he'd better do some serious learning. He wasn't the strongest opponent, but he did learn how to move the pieces with his mouth. Quinn beamed at him as he moved a rook into position. Such a quick study.

Later the two of them sat together and read science textbooks under the big oak tree. Quinn made a special book holder for Otis and turned the pages for him whenever he gave her the throaty signal.

As the sun was setting at the end of their first full day together, Quinn and Otis put on a little hula hoop show for some friends. Otis couldn't really keep a hula hoop in the air with his hips, but he did look adorable with a pair of hoops around his neck. And Quinn was so happy, she was a hula maniac! Being with Otis was better than a successful experiment. It was a dream come true.

Crisis averted, Chase, Logan, Zoey, Lola, and Nicole were hanging out at a pair of tables, shooting the breeze and relaxing at last. Chase was regaling his pals with the stories of some of his more impressive scars.

"And I got this one when I was about seven," he said. "See, I was riding my bike down this insane hill and there was a canteen hanging on the handle bar . . ."

"Ohhhh," Nicole said, entranced. This story sounded like it had a gruesome ending. She loved that.

"And it got caught in my spokes —"

"Hey, guys," a voice called cheerfully.

Chase turned toward the sound and saw Quinn standing there with a shaggy four-legged animal that looked a little like a camel.

"Hey," Zoey replied with a smile. Quinn and Otis were wearing matching purple PCA sweatshirts and both looked happy as clams.

"Hi, Quinn," Nicole greeted with an approving nod. A matched set was always a good idea as far as she was concerned.

"What's up, Otis?" Lola asked, grinning at the fuzzy beast. She saw now why Quinn was so attached. Otis really was adorable.

Logan shook his head. "Uh, did Quinn just walk by here with an alpaca?"

Nicole nodded, impressed that Logan actually knew the difference between an alpaca and a llama. "Uh-huh," she confirmed.

"Yup," Zoey agreed.

"Sure did." Lola looked down at Logan with a casual shrug. Somehow Quinn and her alpaca seemed totally normal to her now.

"Weird," Chase murmured, forgetting all about his scars. He was about to ask how the alpaca got to PCA when the sound of a wailing siren caught his attention. A second later Michael jogged into view, dressed in a blue floral bikini top and green hula skirt. The siren was attached to the flashing light on his head. Chase was all ready to be embarrassed for his friend when he realized that Michael looked . . . happy. He was waving to everyone as he passed, giving the thumbs-up to anyone who looked. He even tousled Logan's hair as he swished by.

"Okay," Nicole said as the sound of the siren faded. "Did Michael just run by here wearing a bikini top?" The blue floral pattern was really cute. If she truly saw what she thought she saw, she would have to ask him if she could borrow it.

"And a hula skirt?" Lola added, looking to her friends for reassurance. Was she seeing things?

"Uh-huh," Chase confirmed as he watched his roommate go. Based on his happy hula, he'd definitely have to say that Michael's first date with Vanessa had gone great.

"He did," Logan echoed.

Zoey shook her head. Alpacas. Guys dressed in bikini tops and hula skirts. It was all in a day at PCA. Man, she loved this place.